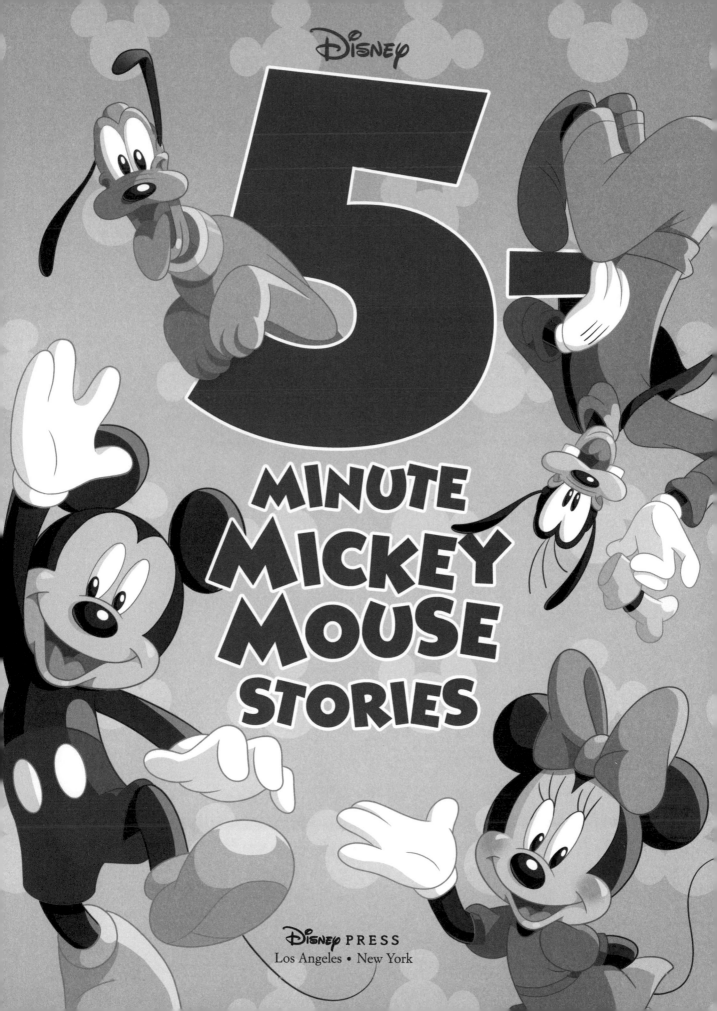

5-MINUTE MICKEY MOUSE STORIES

DISNEY PRESS
Los Angeles • New York

SUSTAINABLE FORESTRY INITIATIVE   Certified Sourcing
www.sfiprogram.org
SFI-00993
Logo Applies to Text Stock Only

Contents

Gone Surfin'   1

A Day at the Park   17

A Sure Cure for the Hiccups   31

Mickey and the Kitten-Sitters   47

The Talent Show   65

A Surprise for Pluto   81

Lost and Found   97

Mickey Mouse and the Pet Show   113

Mickey's Rafting Trip   127

Chef Mickey   141

A Day at the Beach   157

Mickey's Campout   173

Gone Surfin'

It was a perfect day for the beach. The sun was shining, and the water was crystal clear.

Mickey and his friends climbed out of the car and unloaded their surfboards. Goofy was going to teach everyone how to surf!

Mickey couldn't wait to get started. As he looked out at the crashing waves, he pictured himself gliding across them.

"Come on! Let's go!" Mickey called, running into the water.

Boards in hand, Minnie, Donald, and Daisy raced after him.

Goofy chased his friends, the hot sand burning his feet.

"Ooh! Ouch! Wait up," Goofy cried. "Where are you going?"

Donald looked at Goofy, confused. "What do you mean?" he asked.
"We're going to surf!"

"Hyuck," Goofy laughed. "Not yet. You have to learn the basics on
the sand. Come on, I'll show you!"

With Goofy's help, the friends practiced paddling on their surfboards. Then Goofy showed them how to pop up when they reached a wave. But as he leaped up to stand, he lost his balance!

"Whoa!" Goofy cried. He flailed his arms and toppled off the side of his board. "Gawrsh," he said with a laugh, brushing off sand. "That sure was a big wave!"

Lying on her stomach, Minnie placed her hands under her. Then, pushing off, she jumped to stand up on her board, one leg in front of the other.

Goofy clapped. "Good job, Minnie!" he said.

Before long, Donald and Daisy learned to pop up, too. "This is too easy!" Donald complained. "When do we get to go into the water?"

But Mickey wasn't finding it easy at all. He kept losing his balance and falling off his board!

Mickey wiped sweat from his brow. "Gosh, Goof. This is harder than it looks!" he said. "I keep falling over."

"That's okay, Mickey," Goofy said. "Falling is part of surfing. Try this!"

Goofy showed Mickey how to get on his knees on the surfboard before popping up. Pretty soon, Mickey got the hang of it.

"Way to go!" Minnie said, patting him on the back.

Meanwhile, Donald was getting more and more impatient. "Surfing on sand is boring!" he said, stomping his foot. "I want to go in the water!"

Goofy looked out at the ocean. "I'm ready if you are!" he said. "Let's catch some waves!"

But surfing was much harder on water than on sand. Donald tried to surf a wave . . . and plunged into the ocean.

Just when Daisy thought she was surfing—*splash!*—she tumbled into the ocean, too. "Ptooey!" She spit water from her beak.

Minnie was the first to find her balance. Her friends cheered as she crested a wave. After a while, Daisy shakily got up on her board, too. "Cowabunga!" she exclaimed.

Donald was tired of crashing. "This is taking forever!" he said. But finally, he rode a wave, too. "I'm doing it!" he said before tipping back into the water.

Meanwhile, Mickey wasn't having very much luck. He couldn't stay on his board! Every time he popped up, he toppled over and wiped out!

"Phew!" said Mickey. He needed a break! Learning to surf wasn't easy, but Mickey wasn't going to give up.

Just then, Goofy floated by, relaxing on his board and soaking up the rays.

"Hey, Goof," Mickey called. "I'm having a little trouble! How about some one-on-one help?"

"Of course, Mickey!" Goofy said. "That's what friends are for!"

"Thanks!" Mickey said.

"I know just how you feel. When I started surfing, I didn't think I'd ever figure it out!" Goofy said. "I still fall sometimes. But so does every surfer!"

Mickey took Goofy's words to heart. He was up for the challenge!

Goofy and Mickey practiced paddling. They practiced popping up. They even practiced keeping their balance on the board.

Soon Mickey saw a big wave headed his way. He paddled toward the wave, and before he knew it . . .

. . . he was surfing!

Mickey's friends clapped and cheered.

"You're doing it!" Minnie shouted.

"Hooray!" yelled Donald and Daisy.

Goofy was celebrating loudest of all. "I knew you could do it, Mickey!" he shouted.

Mickey loved the feeling of surfing! It was just like he'd imagined.

Learning hadn't been easy, but the hard work had been worth it. And having friends to cheer him on made it that much sweeter!

A Day at the Park

One sunny afternoon, Mickey and his nephews headed to Wonder World, the best amusement park around. For weeks Morty and Ferdie had been begging their uncle to take them.

"Here it is, boys!" said Mickey. "Are you ready for a day full of rides and games?"

"Yes!" the boys shouted together. They could hardly wait to get through the gates!

"Wait until you try out the bumper cars," Mickey said as they walked into the park. "They're my favorite ride here! Now come on. What should we do first?"

"I'm going right to the teacups!" said Ferdie excitedly.

"I'm going right to the swings!" Morty said, jumping up and down.

Mickey laughed. "Well, we can't do two things at the same time, so let's—"

But Morty and Ferdie weren't listening. The two ran off in opposite directions!

"Boys! Boys! Come back!" Mickey yelled after them. But the boys were already too far away to hear him.

Mickey ran after
Morty, but his nephew was
already out of sight. Where could
he have gone? What had he said he wanted to do first?

"The swings!" Mickey said, running toward the ride.

Mickey craned his neck, trying to see if Morty was on the ride. It was way above his head, going around and around. All he could see were feet! He watched for a few minutes, but he didn't think he saw his nephew.

I guess I'll go look for Ferdie, Mickey thought.

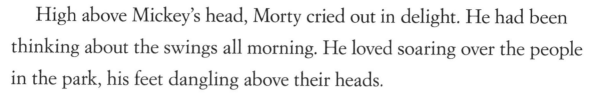

High above Mickey's head, Morty cried out in delight. He had been thinking about the swings all morning. He loved soaring over the people in the park, his feet dangling above their heads.

Suddenly, Morty spotted his uncle Mickey.

"Hi, Uncle Mickey!" he shouted. But he was too far up for his uncle to hear him.

As Mickey ran to the other side of the park, he tried to remember what Ferdie had wanted to do. Then he spotted it: the teacups!

Mickey watched as the giant cups spun around and around. He looked into each cup as it passed by him, but he didn't see Ferdie anywhere. And just watching the ride was making Mickey dizzy! He decided to try another direction.

Where should I look next? he thought.

Inside a teacup, Ferdie grabbed the wheel in the middle. He pulled hard to spin himself around faster and faster. *Whoosh* went the wind across his face as he whipped around. Ferdie laughed. He wished Morty and Uncle Mickey were there to join in the fun!

Mickey was starting to get worried. Where could his nephews be?
He looked everywhere, but he couldn't find the boys. They weren't
on the Ferris wheel. They weren't on the roller coaster. They weren't
riding the carousel. They weren't even playing any of the games.

Finally, Mickey stumbled upon a huge crowd of people. *What's going on?* he wondered. He peeked through the people and saw a parade winding down the path. There were floats, a marching band, dancers . . . even clowns.

Morty and Ferdie would never miss this! he thought. He began to search for them in the crowd. But the boys were nowhere to be found.

Mickey glumly sat down on a bench and watched people walking by. Suddenly, he heard someone calling his name.

"Uncle Mickey!"

Morty and Ferdie, loaded down with snacks, ran up to Mickey.

"We've been looking for you everywhere!" said Morty. "Where were you?"

Mickey jumped up and pulled the boys into a huge hug. "*You* were looking for *me*?" he said. "I looked for you all over the park!"

"We're sorry," said Ferdie.

"We were just so excited to try all the rides!" said Morty. "We've done just about everything."

"I was hoping we'd explore the park *together*," said Mickey. "That's part of the fun of coming here."

"Sorry, Uncle Mickey," the boys said. Then they looked at each other and smiled.

"We did save the best part for you, though," said Morty.

Crash! Mickey's bumper car bounced off Ferdie's and straight into Morty's.

"I'll get you for that!" yelled Morty, steering back toward his uncle. Mickey drove his car out of the way, causing Morty to bump into Ferdie instead. All three of them laughed.

"You were right, Uncle Mickey," said Ferdie.

"Yep! It's way more fun to do this together!" agreed Morty.

Mickey smiled and drove his car right into his nephews' cars—*BONK!*

A Sure Cure for the Hiccups

Mickey sighed. He had been hiccupping all morning. And it was very hard to paint shutters with the hiccups! Every time Mickey picked up his brush—

"*Hic!*" His body shook and paint flew everywhere.

Minnie was passing by and noticed that Mickey looked upset. "What's wrong?" she asked.

"Oh, hiya—*hic!*—Minnie," Mickey replied. "It's nothing. *Hic!* I just can't seem—*hic!*—to get rid of these hiccups!"

Minnie invited Mickey next door. Inside, she poured him a glass of water. "Take a tiny sip," Minnie said. "Then count to five and take another sip."

Mickey gave it a try. But the hiccups just kept coming.

"Hmmm," said Minnie. "Try it with your eyes closed."

Mickey closed his eyes and took a sip. "One, two, three, four—*hic!*"

Just then, there was a knock at Minnie's door. Daisy had come over for their daily walk.

"Hiya—*hic!*—Daisy," said Mickey. *"Hic! Hic!"*

"Wow," Daisy said, coming inside. "It sounds like you need my tried-and-true hiccup cure! It may seem silly, but it will take your mind off your hiccups. Just do what I do."

Daisy stood on her tiptoes. Mickey did, too. Daisy twirled out Minnie's front door. Mickey did, too.

Daisy did two high kicks, tap-danced down the front walk, spun around once, and took a bow.

Mickey wasn't sure he could do all that. But he was willing to *try* anything. So he high-kicked, tap-danced, and spun right to Daisy's side.

"Good job, Mickey!" Daisy said. "How are your hiccups?"

Mickey's face brightened. "Hey!" he shouted. "I think they're gone! Thanks, Daisy. You're the—*hic!*" Mickey frowned. "I guess they're not gone after all."

"Hmmm," said Daisy. "Maybe Donald knows a good cure for hiccups. Let's go ask him."

The three friends set out to find Donald. But Minnie and Daisy were much faster than Mickey. When he arrived at Donald's house, they were waiting by the front door.

"Where's Donald?" Mickey asked.

Before Daisy could answer, Donald jumped out at Mickey.

"Aaaaaaah!" Mickey cried.

"Sorry, Mickey," Donald said. "Daisy and Minnie said you have the hiccups. I thought maybe I could scare them away."

Minnie, Daisy, and Donald watched Mickey closely. "Did it work?" Minnie asked.

But Mickey just hiccupped again.

"Aw, phooey," Donald said.

Mickey tried everything he could think of to get rid of his hiccups. He stood on his head while saying the alphabet backward. *"Hic!"*

He held his nose and whistled a tune while hopping on one foot. *"Hic!"*

He skipped rope and sang, "M, my name is Mickey—*hic!*—I have a friend named Minnie—*hic!*—and I like mints! *Hic! Hic!*"

Mickey sat down in Donald's hammock and moped. He was starting to feel like he would never get rid of his hiccups. "It's no use," he said to his friends. "I think my hiccups are—*hic!*—here to stay."

Daisy led Minnie and Donald to the side of the yard. The three of them whispered to one another for several minutes. They had to find a way to help Mickey! Finally, Donald rushed inside and returned with a large sack.

Donald reached into the sack and pulled out some blocks. Concentrating hard, he balanced three of them on his bill!

Next Minnie and Daisy pulled two hoops out of the sack. They hung one on each of Donald's arms, and he began to twirl them.

"Okay, Mickey!" Donald said. "Now you try!"

Mickey wanted to try, but all he could do was laugh! "I'm sorry, Donald," he said between giggles. "You just look so . . . silly!"

"Silly?!" Donald said crossly. "You call this silly?"

Mickey just laughed harder.

When he finally stopped laughing, Mickey realized something. His hiccups were gone. He and his friends waited and waited—but not another hiccup came!

"I did it!" Donald cried. "I cured Mickey!"

"You sure did, Donald," Mickey said. "I guess laughter really *is* the best medicine—for hiccups!"

Mickey and the Kitten-Sitters

"**G**uess what?" Mickey Mouse said to his nephews, Morty and Ferdie. "We're going to watch Minnie's kitten, Figaro, while she visits her cousin. Isn't that exciting?"

Before Morty and Ferdie could answer, they heard wild clucking, flapping, and crowing coming from next door. Suddenly, Pluto raced across the lawn. A big, angry rooster followed close behind him.

"Pluto!" Minnie scolded. "Chasing chickens again! Aren't you ashamed?"

Pluto *was* a bit ashamed, but only because he had let the rooster bully him.

"It's a good thing Figaro is staying with you," Minnie told Mickey as she got into her car. "Maybe he can teach Pluto how to behave!"

Minnie was hardly out of sight when Figaro leaped out of Mickey's arms and scampered into the kitchen. With one quick hop, he jumped onto the table and knocked over a pitcher of cream.

Pluto growled at the kitten, but Mickey just cleaned up the mess.

"Take it easy, Pluto," he said. "Figaro is our guest."

At dinnertime, Pluto ate his food the way a good dog should. But no matter how hard Mickey and the boys tried, Figaro wouldn't touch the special food Minnie had left for him.

At bedtime, Figaro would not use the cushion Minnie had brought for him. Instead, he got into bed with Ferdie and tickled his ears. Finally, he bounced off to the kitchen.

"Uncle Mickey," called Morty. "Did you remember to close the kitchen window?"

"Oh, no!" cried Mickey, jumping out of bed. The kitchen window was open, and Figaro was nowhere to be seen.

Mickey and the boys searched the entire house. They looked
upstairs and downstairs, under every chair, and even in the yard. But
they couldn't find the little kitten anywhere.

"You two stay here," Mickey told his nephews. "Pluto and I will
find Figaro."

Mickey and Pluto went to Minnie's house first, but Figaro wasn't there. Next they went to the park down the street.

"Have you seen a little black-and-white kitten?" Mickey asked a policeman.

"I certainly have!" answered the policeman. "He was teasing the ducks by the pond!"

Mickey and Pluto hurried to the pond. Figaro wasn't there, but they *did* find some small, muddy footprints.

Mickey and Pluto followed the trail of footprints to Main Street, where they met a grocery truck driver.

"Have you seen a kitten?" Mickey asked.

"Have I!" cried the driver. "He knocked over my eggs!"

Mickey groaned as he paid for the eggs. Where was Figaro?

Mickey and Pluto searched the whole town, but there was no sign of the kitten. By the time they returned home, the sun was starting to rise.

Soon Minnie drove up. "Where is Figaro?" she asked.

No one answered.

"Something has happened to him!" Minnie cried. "Can't I trust you to watch *one* sweet little kitten?"

Just then, there was a loud clucking from the yard next door. A dozen frantic hens came flapping over the fence, with Figaro close behind.

"There's your sweet little kitten!" exclaimed Mickey. "He ran away last night and teased the ducks in the park. Then he broke the eggs in the grocery truck and—"

"And now he's chasing chickens!" Minnie finished.

"I had hoped Figaro would teach Pluto some manners," Minnie said. "Instead, Pluto has been teaching him to misbehave!"

"Pluto didn't do anything wrong," Ferdie said.

But Minnie wouldn't listen. She picked up Figaro and quickly drove away.

"Don't worry, boys," said Mickey. "We'll tell her the whole story later, when she's not so upset."

"Please don't tell her too soon," begged Morty. "As long as Aunt Minnie thinks Pluto is a bad dog, we won't have to kitten-sit Figaro."

Mickey smiled and said, "Maybe we *should* wait a little while. We could all use some peace and quiet." And with that, he and Pluto settled down for a well-deserved nap.

The Talent Show

Mickey Mouse sighed as he looked out the window. It was pouring outside.

"Sorry, gang," he said. "It doesn't look like we'll be able to go for a hike today after all!"

"Now what are we going to do?" Donald asked.

"I have an idea!" Minnie said. "Let's put on a talent show. We can have it right here."

"And we can invite all our friends!" added Mickey.

Donald had a great idea for an act—but he couldn't do it alone.

"Hey, Pluto! Want to be in my act?" he asked.

Pluto barked happily.

"Great!" Donald replied. He dashed to the kitchen. A few minutes later he came back carrying a large bowl of fruit.

Everyone was curious about Donald's props, but he didn't want to ruin the surprise. "Come on, Pluto!" he said. "Let's go practice in the attic."

Donald waited until they were all alone to tell Pluto about his big idea. "We're going to have the best act in the talent show!" he exclaimed. "I'm going to juggle this fruit. Then I'll throw it to you one piece at a time so you can balance it on your nose."

Donald grabbed an apple, a peach, and a pear. "Watch this!" he said.

Donald tossed the fruit into the air and started to juggle. Pluto was so impressed that he sat back and barked his approval.

"Good! You sit—just like that!" Donald told Pluto. "Now I'll throw the fruit over . . . one at a time. Okay? One . . . two . . . *three!*"

Just as Donald tossed the peach to Pluto, the attic door creaked open.

Pluto spun around to see who was there. The peach sailed past his head and landed on thc floor with a juicy *splat*!

"I just wanted to see if you'd like to help invite our friends to the talent show," Daisy said, holding up a phone.

"Can't you see we're practicing?" Donald snapped. Then he closed the door—right in Daisy's face.

Donald picked up the smashed peach. "Yuck!" he said. "I can't juggle with this!"

Donald plucked a plum from the fruit bowl and started juggling again. The fruits went *whoosh—whoosh—whoosh* through the air.

This time, when Donald tossed the plum into the air, Pluto was ready. He caught it on his nose!

"Great job!" Donald cheered. "Okay, here comes the pear. . . ."

Knock-knock-knock!

Pluto and Donald jumped!

The plum rolled off Pluto's nose, and Donald dropped the pear and the apple accidentally. All the fruit went *splat*!

"Hi there, Donald! Howdy, Pluto! Wow, it looks like you're working really hard!" Mickey said. "I can't wait to—"

"What do you want?" Donald grumbled.

"We're almost ready to go on," Mickey replied. "I was wondering if you'd like to help decorate the set!"

"We don't have time for that!" Donald said. "Can't you see we're practicing?"

"Oh," Mickey said. "Sorry to bother you."

Donald took a deep breath and picked up another apple. "It's almost time for the show," he said, "and we *still* haven't practiced all the way through!"

Pluto looked worried.

"It's okay, Pluto," Donald continued. "I'm good at juggling things, and *you're* good at catching things. I'm sure it will be—"

Just then, Minnie poked her head into the attic. "Does anybody need help with their costumes?" she asked.

"No!" Donald hollered. "What we need is *practice*—and no more interruptions!"

"I'm sorry," Minnie replied. "But Mickey also asked me to give you a message. The show is about to start!"

Donald peeked out the attic window. Sure enough, he could see Huey, Dewey, and Louie dodging raindrops as they hurried to the house.

"Good luck with your last practice," Minnie said in a small voice before she slipped out the door.

Donald glanced at the fruit bowl. It had looked so full before, but now there were only a prickly pineapple, a watermelon, and a bunch of bananas left. There was barely enough fruit to juggle in the show, let alone to practice with.

When they went downstairs, Donald and Pluto could see how hard everyone had worked to get ready for the talent show. Donald wondered how they'd had time to practice their own acts.

"I'm sorry," Donald said. "I should've helped everybody get ready—instead of yelling at you for interrupting my rehearsal."

Mickey smiled and stepped in front of the audience. "Welcome, friends, to the Rainy Day Talent Show!" he announced.

Donald watched as his friends shared their acts. First Mickey performed an amazing magic trick. Then Minnie did a special dance. Next Daisy played a song on her harmonica.

"You're up!" Mickey told Donald and Pluto. "Break a leg!"

Donald and Pluto walked to the center of the stage. As Pluto sat back on his haunches, Donald grabbed the bunch of bananas.

But Donald had never juggled with a bunch of bananas before! The bananas flew across the room, making the whole audience laugh.

Donald's cheeks turned pink as he grabbed the pineapple and tossed it into the air. "Ouch—oof—ow—ugh!" Donald exclaimed as he tried to juggle it. He glanced at Pluto, who shook his head and hid under his paws.

Soon only the watermelon was left. When Pluto saw Donald reach for it, he hid under the couch!

The audience howled with laughter.

Too embarrassed and upset to face his friends, Donald rushed off the stage.

Pluto nuzzled his hand. A few minutes later, Mickey, Minnie, and Daisy joined them.

"What's wrong, Donald?" Daisy asked.

Donald stared at her in amazement. "What's *wrong*?" he said.

"Everything! My act was a disaster! It made everyone laugh and turned me into a big joke!"

"Actually," Mickey said, "you and Pluto were the stars of the show!"

"That's right," Minnie agreed. "We wanted to entertain our friends, and you did. Everyone's having a great time!"

"In fact, I can still hear them clapping," Mickey added.

Donald couldn't believe it, but Mickey was right. Everyone *was* clapping!

"You'd better get out there and give them an encore," Mickey told him.

"I don't have enough fruit," Donald said. "Pineapples and watermelons were not made for juggling!"

"How about you juggle balls instead?" Daisy suggested.

"And we'll save the fruit for fruit salad!" Minnie said, giggling.

A Surprise for Pluto

One sunny morning, Mickey Mouse looked out the window. "What a beautiful day!" he exclaimed. "This is perfect building weather."

His nephews, Morty and Ferdie, joined him. "What are you going to build, Uncle Mickey?" asked Morty.

Mickey's eyes twinkled. "Oh, I don't know," he said. "Maybe . . . a tree house!"

The boys jumped up and down. "A tree house?" Ferdie said.

"Can we help?" Morty asked.

"You would be great helpers," Mickey replied. "But there will be lots of tools in the yard. It might not be very safe. Why don't you take Pluto to the park instead?"

"Sure, Uncle Mickey!" the boys replied.

With Morty, Ferdie, and Pluto gone, Mickey called his friends.
He told them all about the tree house and asked if they would like
to help.

Soon Minnie, Donald, Daisy, and Goofy arrived in Mickey's yard.

"Building a tree house is a big job," Mickey said. "Maybe we should split up the work."

"Great idea, Mickey," Goofy said.

"Why don't you saw the boards, Goofy," Mickey said. "Then Donald and I can hammer them together."

Minnie showed Mickey a special drawing she had made.

"Good thinking, Minnie!" Mickey said. "That will be one of the most important jobs of all."

Goofy dumped out his toolbox in a corner of the yard. The tools made a big crash—and a big mess! Goofy found what he was looking for and began sawing the boards.

After a few minutes, Minnie walked up to him. "Sorry to bother you, Goofy," she began. "I was wondering if you would cut some boards for me, too."

"Sure!" Goofy said with a grin. "Just tell me what you need."

Over by the big tree, Donald and Mickey worked together to make
a rope ladder. When they were finished, Mickey attached
the ladder to the thickest branch. He gave the ladder a strong tug. It
didn't budge.

"That should do it," Mickey said. "Once we finish building,
we can use this ladder to climb into the tree house."

Just then, Goofy brought them a stack of boards. "Here you go!" he said proudly. "I still have to saw the boards for the roof, but you can use these for the floor and the walls."

"Thanks, Goofy!" Mickey said.

Mickey and Donald climbed into the tree, pulling the boards behind them. The sounds of their hammers echoed through the backyard as the friends started building.

Across the yard, Minnie pulled her hammer out of her tool belt. As she picked up the first board, she realized that she had forgotten something very important.

Minnie hurried over to the big tree. "Do you have any extra nails?" she called up. "I left all of mine at home!"

"I have some," Donald said. He fished a box of nails out of his tool belt and gave them to Minnie.

On the way back to her project, Minnie stopped to see how Daisy was doing.

"Wow, Daisy," Minnie said. "You mixed up a lot of paint!"

Daisy giggled. "I might have mixed a little *too* much," she said. "Do you need any paint for your project?"

"Thanks, Daisy," Minnie said. "That would be great!"

Soon everyone was hard at work.

Buzz-buzz-buzz went the saw.

Bang-bang-bang went the hammers.

Swish-swish-swish went the paintbrushes.

Mickey's backyard was a very busy place!

Later that day, Morty, Ferdie, and Pluto came home from the park. Morty and Ferdie couldn't believe their eyes. "Wow!" the boys cried.

"This is the best tree house ever!" added Ferdie as they scrambled up the rope ladder.

Beneath them, Pluto whined. He couldn't climb the ladder like the others.

Mickey understood right away. "Don't worry, Pluto!" he called.
"Come around to the other side of the tree."

Pluto trotted around the tree and found something that made his
tail wag: a set of stairs that was just his size!

"Minnie made them for you," Mickey explained. "Now come
on up and join the fun!"

Pluto ran up the stairs. It really *was* the best tree house ever!

Lost and Found

One spring morning, Mickey woke up and looked outside. It was a perfect day. The sky was blue, the air was fresh, and a gentle breeze blew through the trees. Mickey smiled to himself. A day like that meant only one thing: an adventure was in order!

There was just one problem. Mickey didn't know what he wanted to do!

Mickey sat down to think. What should he do with his day? Then he sat up straight. He could work in the garden! He could plant some more flowers and vegetables so that his garden would be complete. Then Mickey let out a sigh. That wouldn't work. He didn't have any seeds.

Mickey went back to thinking. Suddenly, he sat up straight again. He had it this time—the perfect idea! He could go to the farmers market and pick up something sweet for Minnie. Mickey looked down at his watch and sighed. It was too early. The farmers market wasn't open yet.

Just then, Mickey heard a noise in his front yard. Walking to the window, he saw his friend Goofy sitting on a bike.

"Hiya, Mickey!" Goofy called. "Want to go for a ride?"

"That's a great idea!" Mickey said happily. "I'd love to!"

Mickey laughed. He hadn't had to come up with an adventure—the adventure had come to him!

Mickey grabbed his own bike, and he and Goofy headed off down the road.

As they turned onto the bike path, Mickey looked around. Everywhere he looked, there were signs of spring. The friends passed by a field full of bright yellow flowers that filled the air with a wonderful smell.

"Look!" Mickey exclaimed as they rode farther down the road. "Up in that tree!" In the branches, a family of birds was making a nest. They chirped happily as they fluttered back and forth.

Mickey was so busy looking at the birds that he didn't notice a
large branch on the path in front of him. As he rode over the branch,
his tires began to wobble. Then his handlebars began to wobble. Soon
he had lost control of his bike! Before he could even let out a shout,
Mickey flew off the path and careened into the woods.

On the path, Goofy kept pedaling. He had no idea that Mickey
was no longer with him.

Mickey bounced and bumped his way over rocks and sticks until, finally, he got control of his bike. He came to a stop, climbed off his bike, and took a look around.

He was in a part of the woods he had never been in before. Mickey shivered as he realized something: he was lost!

"I'd better figure out how to get back to the path," Mickey said to himself. "I don't want Goofy to worry about me." Just then, Mickey heard a rustling behind him. "And I'm not so sure I want to be out here alone, either!"

Mickey jumped onto his bike and began to pedal back toward the path. Or at least, he *hoped* he was going toward the path. But the farther he pedaled, the wilder the woods around him grew.

At first, Mickey was nervous. Biking through the woods wasn't the same as biking on the path. But as he went, Mickey couldn't help noticing that it was beautiful in its own way.

"This isn't so bad," Mickey said. "It's actually kind of pretty. And the animals aren't all that scary." Mickey waved hello to a mother possum carrying her babies on her back. He spotted a hedgehog, some squirrels, even a fox. He waved hello to them, too.

The one thing Mickey didn't see was the path home.

As Mickey looked around the forest, he had a thought. The day was probably half over! He didn't want to get stuck in the woods after dark. Possums and hedgehogs were cute, but what kind of animals would he run into at night?

Mickey began to pedal faster.

And then he stopped short.

There, right in front of him, was a picture-perfect pond!

Mickey put his finger to his chin. He was thinking—but this time it wasn't about where to go for the day. He had just found the perfect place to go any day!

"This would be a great place for a picnic!" he shouted happily. "I can't wait to tell Goofy!"

He took one last look at the pond and turned around. He was more determined than ever to get back on the path and find Goofy.

Mickey pedaled and pedaled. Soon the forest grew thinner. Then, almost as quickly as he had gone off the path, he found himself back on it.

Suddenly, Goofy rounded the corner. "Mickey!" he shouted, startled to see his friend ahead of him. "Weren't you behind me?"

Mickey laughed. Goofy hadn't even known he was gone. "I got lost!" he said. "I've been riding through the woods this whole time! Wait till you hear what I found!"

As they rode back home, Mickey told his friend all about the pond. "There's a rock where we can lay out our picnic," he said. "And there's a perfect branch for a rope swing."

Together, Mickey and Goofy went to the farmers market. They grabbed sandwiches and fruit and gathered it together in a picnic basket. They bought a big blanket to sit on. Then Mickey stopped by the flower shop and got some flowers to take with him.

The only thing left to do was get their friends. Mickey and Goofy gathered everyone together and led them to the path. "Come on," Mickey said. "I have a surprise for you!"

He led them through the woods—which didn't seem nearly as scary with his friends by his side—and straight to the pond.

"It turns out I needed to get lost to find this place!" Mickey said. "But I'm sure glad I did."

The others agreed. Mickey had found them their new favorite swimming spot!

Mickey Mouse and the Pet Show

It was a perfect day for a cookout. Mickey Mouse and his nephews, Morty and Ferdie, were preparing lunch.

Pluto barked a friendly welcome to Minnie as she joined the boys in the yard.

"I'm sorry I'm late," she said, "but I have great news. I've just been elected chairperson of the Charity Pet Show. We're raising money to build a new shelter for stray animals."

"We should enter Pluto in the show!" Morty suggested.

"Yeah! We can teach him to do tricks," said Ferdie. "Can we, Uncle Mickey? Please?"

"All right," Mickey said. "It's for a good cause."

Mickey and Minnie watched as the boys started to train Pluto.

"Roll over, Pluto," Morty said.

But Pluto just sat up and wagged his tail.

"Maybe we should show him what we want him to do," said Ferdie.
Pluto watched, puzzled, as both boys rolled over in the grass.
"Let's try something that *he* likes to do," suggested Morty.
Ferdie ordered Pluto to lie down, but Pluto jumped up and began chasing his tail instead.

All week long, Morty and Ferdie tried to teach Pluto new tricks. He fetched, rolled over, lay down, begged, and shook hands . . . but only when *he* wanted to.

"Well, he *is* doing tricks," said Mickey.

"They're just not the *right* tricks," said Ferdie.

"He'll never win first prize," said Morty.

On the day of the show, Mickey and the boys took Pluto to the empty lot next door, where the show was being held. Minnie sold Mickey three tickets, then pointed happily to the cashbox.

"We've made enough to pay for the new animal shelter!" she told him.

"That's great!" cried Mickey.

What *wasn't* great was Pluto's performance.

He shook hands when he was told to sit. He rolled over when he should have jumped. He barked when he was supposed to lie down. Worst of all, when Police Chief O'Hara was choosing Best Pet of the Day, Pluto growled at him! The chief didn't know it, but he was standing right where Pluto had buried his bone!

Suddenly, the crowd heard a scream from the ticket booth.

"Help! Stop, thief! Help!"

"That's Minnie!" Mickey gasped.

"The ticket money!" Morty and Ferdie shouted.

Mickey, the boys, and Chief O'Hara ran to the booth.

Pluto was already at the scene of the crime. He was busily
sniffing around.

"All the money is gone," Minnie said. "I walked away for one
minute. When I came back, I saw someone running away with
the cashbox."

"What did the robber look like?" asked the chief.

Before Minnie could answer, Pluto took off. A moment later, the thief ran screaming out of the woods. He was holding on to the cashbox—and Pluto was holding on to him! Pluto growled and tugged on the thief's suspenders.

Snap! The thief's suspenders broke and shot him right into the arms of Chief O'Hara.

Later that afternoon, Chief O'Hara presented Pluto with the Four-Footed Hero medal.

The chief smiled and said, "Thanks to Pluto, every animal will have a place to go—and a chance to find a good home."

At home, Pluto waited by the front door.

"You know," said Morty, "I don't care if Pluto isn't a show dog. He's something better. He's a *hero* dog."

Mickey, Minnie, and Ferdie agreed. Then, without being told,
Pluto shook hands with everyone, because this time *he* wanted to.

Mickey's Rafting Trip

One sunny summer's day, Mickey, Minnie, and Pluto headed deep into the woods.

"I can't wait to get to the river," Minnie said. "Going white-water rafting is such an adventure!"

Pluto barked in agreement.

"Well, you don't have to wait much longer," Mickey said, pointing through the trees. "Look! There's the river!"

When they reached the water, Mickey inflated the raft while
Pluto unpacked the oars. Minnie secured all their gear for the trip
downriver. Then the three friends put on their helmets and climbed
into the raft. The water was shallow and still.

"One, two, three, push!" Mickey yelled. He and Minnie pushed
away from the shore with their oars. Then they paddled through the
calm water toward the rapids.

When they reached the fast-moving water, Mickey and Minnie worked together to move the raft safely through the choppy waves.

"Paddle on the left!" Minnie yelled to Mickey over the roaring river.

Mickey moved his oar to the left side and pulled it hard through the water. The little raft veered around a rock.

Pluto sat in the middle of the raft, watching the forest rush by and loving the ride.

The trio swished and bumped and sloshed their way down the river. Suddenly, Pluto stood and started barking.

"What is it, boy?" Mickey asked. He and Minnie both looked in the direction that Pluto was barking.

"Oh, Mickey, look! There's a bear cub stuck on that rock!" cried Minnie.

Just ahead of them, a sopping wet bear cub stood shivering on a large rock in the middle of the river. He looked cold and scared.

"We have to help him!" Minnie said. "But the raft is headed away from him."

"Quick!" Mickey said. "Paddle on the right!"

The two friends pulled their oars hard, turning the raft toward the little bear.

Mickey jumped out and pulled the raft near the rock.

"Hi, little guy," he said, turning to the bear cub. "How did you get stuck out here?"

"Bears like to swim," Minnie said. "Maybe this cub is too young to be a strong swimmer and the current pulled him out here."

"Let's get him in the raft. We'll take him back to the shore to find his family," Mickey said.

Nudging him gently, Mickey moved the bear cub toward the raft. The cub was nervous, but he seemed to trust his new friends. He stepped into the boat and sat down next to Pluto.

"All right, here we go!" Mickey said as he stepped in. He and Minnie used their oars to push away from the rock and back into the rapids.

"Look for a good place to land on the shore!" Minnie yelled to Mickey over the rushing water.

The forest was thick along the river. Mickey and Minnie searched for a beach or another flat rock so they could safely land the raft. They passed trees, bushes, and rocky cliffs as they sped through the waves.

The raft bounced and plunged. The bear cub snuggled close to Pluto, hiding his face.

"I see a spot!" Minnie said. "There's a little beach just ahead!"

Soon they were safely on the shore. The bear cub leaped from the
raft. He jumped and rolled in the sand, then ran back and forth in
front of Mickey, Minnie, and Pluto.

"He's probably the first bear ever to try white-water rafting!"
Mickey said, laughing.

"I don't think he liked it as much as we do! Look how happy he is
to be back on land," Minnie said.

"What should we do now?" Minnie asked. "We can't just leave him here. We're so far downriver from where we found him! What if he doesn't know how to get home?"

"I suppose we can walk back through the woods to help him find his family," Mickey said, "as long as you don't mind cutting our rafting trip short."

The friends agreed that was a good plan, and they packed up all their supplies.

Mickey, Minnie, Pluto, and the bear cub headed through the forest, following the winding path of the river. They climbed rocks, jumped over fallen logs, and crossed through streams. Pluto and the cub ran ahead, chasing each other around the trees.

"The sounds of the woods are so different from the roaring of the river!" Minnie said. "I can hear birds singing, crickets chirping, and the trickle of the little stream. It's so quiet and peaceful."

Finally, the group reached a little clearing with a rocky cliff on one side. The bear cub ran toward a cave at the base of the cliff.

"Look!" said Minnie. "I think we found his family."

A mama bear and two cubs ran out of the cave toward the little cub. The four licked and nuzzled one another happily.

The little cub turned back toward Mickey, Minnie, and Pluto. They smiled and waved at him from the edge of the clearing.

"Good luck, little guy!" Mickey said.

"Be careful near the river!" Minnie called.

Pluto barked good-bye, and the three friends walked into the woods while the cub followed his family into the cave.

"I'm glad we helped that little cub," Minnie said. "He looked so happy to be home."

"I know we planned to spend the day white-water rafting," Mickey said, "but I think we ended up on an even greater adventure!"

"Yes," Minnie said. "Two adventures are definitely greater than one!"

Chef Mickey

Mickey was excited. He was cooking a romantic dinner for Minnie. He wanted everything to be perfect. There was just one problem. . . . Mickey didn't know what to make!

Maybe my friends will have some ideas, Mickey thought.

Mickey called Donald and Goofy. The friends agreed to come over and help.

Soon Donald and Goofy arrived. They had brought Daisy to help, too!

"What should I make?" Mickey asked his friends.

"Hmmm . . . Minnie likes lasagna," said Daisy.

Daisy was right. Minnie *loved* lasagna. Mickey nodded and started to gather the ingredients.

But Donald had a different idea. "You should make a turkey," he said. "It's Minnie's favorite. That will show her how well you know her!"

"How about a salad?" Goofy added.

Mickey was confused. Daisy was right, but Donald was right, too. And a salad *did* sound good. What was he going to do?

Mickey looked at the ingredients he had taken out. What if he chose wrong?

"What do you think I should do, Pluto?" he asked.

"Woof, woof," Pluto barked.

"You're right," Mickey said. "I *should* make them all!"

Soon Mickey was busy making turkey *and* lasagna *and* salad. It was a lot of food, but he was sure Minnie would love it!

Mickey looked at the clock. It was getting late! He still needed to set the table, but he was too busy cooking.

"I can help you, Mickey," Daisy said.

Daisy pulled out plates and glasses. Then she set the table, decorating it in all Minnie's favorite colors.

Meanwhile, Goofy prepared a special fruit punch.

"Gawrsh, this is fun!" he said, spilling punch all over the table as
he stirred.

Finally, the drink was ready. Goofy picked up the punch bowl and
headed to the dining room. He didn't see Donald walking by with
the salad.

CRASH!

Goofy and Donald smacked into each other. Salad flew into the air. Punch spilled all over the floor. And Goofy fell into Daisy's beautiful table.

Hearing all the noise, Mickey raced into the dining room. He could barely believe his eyes. Everyone's hard work was ruined!

"I'm sorry, Mickey," Goofy said. "I didn't mean to ruin everything. I just wanted to help."

"Me too," Donald said. "I wanted everything to be perfect!"

Mickey looked at his sad friends. "It's okay," he said. "I know it was an accident."

With his friends' help, Mickey began to clean up the mess.
Suddenly, he sniffed the air. "Does anyone smell something
burning?" Mickey asked.

Mickey opened the oven. He had been so busy cleaning that he
had forgotten all about the food. Everything was overcooked!

The dining room was still a mess, and now the food was ruined,
too. What was Mickey going to do?

Just then, Minnie walked through the door. "Hi, Mickey," she called sweetly. "I'm here for our special night."

Minnie looked around the messy room. Mickey was holding a burned turkey, her friends were covered in food, and the table was a mess!

"Oh, Mickey. What happened?" Minnie asked.

"I had everything planned out," Mickey told Minnie. "I wanted our night to be special, so I made all of your favorite dishes. Turkey, lasagna, and salad. I even asked Goofy and Donald to help out. But then Goofy dropped the punch, and Donald dropped the salad. After that, I guess things just got out of control."

"It's okay, Mickey," Minnie said. "I love that you wanted everything to be perfect, but that's not what's important. What's important is the time we spend together."

"Aw, shucks, Minnie," Mickey said. "Thanks! But what are we going to do about dinner?"

Minnie smiled. "I have an idea," she said.

Mickey looked at Minnie and smiled. His night wasn't what he had expected, but he was still having fun. And he had learned an important lesson. As long as he was with Minnie, nothing else mattered.

Mickey handed Minnie a slice of pizza. "You're right, Minnie," he said. "This *is* the perfect night after all."

A Day at the Beach

"**C**ome on, boys. Let's go!" Mickey called. He and Minnie had planned a big surprise for Mickey's nephews, Morty and Ferdie.

"Are we going to play ball?" Morty guessed.

"Or maybe fly a kite?" asked Ferdie.

"Even better! We're going to spend the whole day at the beach!" Mickey announced.

"Hooray!" the boys cheered. Pluto was so excited that he started chasing his tail.

There was a lot to do to get ready for a day at the beach. Minnie used her bows to make a new tail for the boys' kite while Mickey blew up the beach ball. Morty and Ferdie gathered the sunblock, the beach towels, and all their toys, of course.

"There's just one more thing we have to do before we leave," Minnie said. "Pack our picnic!"

Minnie and Mickey helped the boys make their favorite sandwiches. Then everyone worked together to fill the picnic basket with yummy things to eat.

"Whoops—we can't forget a treat for Pluto!" Minnie giggled as she added a bone to the picnic basket.

When they got to the beach,
Morty and Ferdie helped Mickey
and Minnie unload the car.
Finally, everything was set up.

"Last one in the ocean is a
rotten barnacle!" Mickey called.

Mickey and the boys splashed
in the ocean. Pluto joined in the
fun, too . . . until he got distracted
by a crab!

Meanwhile, Minnie spread out the picnic blanket and opened the basket. "Lunch is ready!" she called to the boys.

Morty raced out of the water and grabbed his sandwich. The smell of cheese, lettuce, tomatoes, and pickles made his mouth water. He was about to take a big bite when suddenly—*whoosh*—his sandwich disappeared!

"Hey!" Ferdie yelled. "That seagull stole your sandwich!"

"My sandwich!" Morty howled.

"I'm sorry, Morty," Minnie replied. "Luckily, we have lots of other food to share."

But Morty just shook his head. "That was my favorite sandwich, though," he said sadly.

Ferdie tugged on Mickey's arm. "Come on, Uncle Mickey," he said. "Let's rescue Morty's sandwich."

"I guess it's worth a try," Mickey said. "Follow that gull!"

"Pluto and I will stay here and guard the rest of our picnic," Minnie said. "Good luck!"

The seagull swooped through the sky, casting a shadow over the sand. Mickey, Morty, and Ferdie charged after it. Near the water, Goofy was building a village of sandcastles.

"Hiya, Mickey!" Goofy called. "Where are you going in such a hurry?"

"We're on a sandwich rescue mission!" Mickey replied as he ran past his friend.

A little farther down the beach, Donald and Daisy were flying kites with Huey, Dewey, and Louie. In the sky, the seagull zigged and zagged through the kite strings. But down on the sand, it was a little harder for Mickey and his nephews to get past them.

"Be careful!" cried Daisy.

"Yeah—watch out for the strings!" Donald added.

"And the sand!" Huey yelled, shielding his eyes as Mickey and his nephews kicked up clouds of sand.

"Look, boys!" Mickey called. "The seagull is headed for the cliffs!"

The seagull glided effortlessly on the ocean breeze. Below, Mickey, Morty, and Ferdie made their way across the tide pools to reach the cliffs. The wet sand slowed them down, squishing and squelching under their feet. Mickey and his nephews tiptoed through the water, careful to avoid stepping on the starfish, clams, and sea anemones. They reached the cliffs just as the seagull disappeared over the rocky ledge.

Mickey, Morty, and Ferdie stared up at the cliff. It seemed very high.

"What do we do now, Uncle Mickey?" Ferdie asked.

"Well," Mickey said, "we can go back to Minnie and Pluto and enjoy the rest of our picnic . . . or we can climb the cliff and keep searching for that seagull."

"Let's climb!" Morty replied. By then he was so hungry he could practically taste his favorite sandwich. He couldn't wait to get it back.

Inch by inch, step by step, Mickey and his nephews scaled the rocky cliff. It was even harder than dodging the sandcastles, slipping through the kite strings, and crossing the tide pools!

Finally, they reached the top of the tallest ridge.

"Hold on a minute, boys," Mickey whispered. "Before we climb over the edge, we need a plan."

"I've already got one," Morty said. "As soon as I see that seagull, I'm going to swoop in and snatch my sandwich—just like it did to me!"

Morty hoisted himself up to the edge of the cliff . . . and froze. The
seagull—and the sandwich—were just inches from Morty's face. But
the seagull wasn't alone. It was perched on the side of a grassy nest next
to three baby gulls! From the way the chicks were squawking, Morty
could tell they were just as hungry as he was. Maybe even hungrier!

Morty watched for a moment as the seagull tossed bits of his
sandwich to her babies. Then he began to climb back down the cliff
to where Mickey and Ferdie were waiting. The seagull needed the
sandwich more than he did.

Back on the beach, Morty told Minnie and Pluto all about the baby seagulls sharing his sandwich.

"What an adventure!" Minnie exclaimed. "But don't worry, Morty. We still have lots of food in our picnic basket. Here, I packed an extra roll. And you can have the cheese from my sandwich."

"Take my pickle!" Mickey offered.

"And my tomato!" Ferdie added.

"Thanks, everybody!" Morty said. He grinned as he took a big bite of his brand-new sandwich. It tasted even better than it looked!

Mickey's Campout

Mickey Mouse and his friends were excited. It was time for their annual campout!

Everyone had an important job. Mickey packed the tents. Goofy learned how to build a fire. Minnie and Daisy made dinner. And Donald bought some new flashlights.

"Is everybody ready?" Mickey asked when they had packed up the car. "Let's go!"

Mickey drove up a mountain and through the woods. Finally, he parked the car next to a lake. "Here we are!" he said.

"Gosh, smell that fresh air!" Goofy said as he took a deep breath. "What should we do first?"

"Let's set up our tents," Mickey suggested.

"I've never put up a tent before," Minnie said.

"It's easy!" Mickey told her. "Just slip the tent poles into the pockets."

"Um, Mickey?" Daisy said. "Where are the poles?"

Mickey's eyes grew wide. "Oh, no!" he exclaimed. "I forgot them!"

"That's okay, Mickey," Goofy said. "We'll have just as much fun sleeping under the stars."

As the sun started to set, Daisy shivered. "It's getting a little chilly," she said.

"Maybe we should build a campfire," Donald suggested.

"Sure!" Goofy replied. "Let's go find some firewood."

Mickey and his friends hiked into the forest to gather some firewood. When they had enough, Goofy showed them how to pile the sticks inside a circle of rocks.

"Stand back while I light the fire, everybody," Goofy said. Then he frowned. "Uh-oh. I forgot to bring the matches!"

"Don't worry, Goofy," Minnie said. "Our sleeping bags will keep us warm. Now, who's hungry? We have hot dogs, corn—"

"And s'mores for dessert!" added Daisy.

But Minnie and Daisy found a big surprise when they reached the picnic basket: the basket had tipped over and something had eaten all the food!

"No tents, no campfire, and no dinner," grumbled Donald. "At least we have flashlights!"

Click.

Donald pushed the button on the flashlight, but it didn't shine.

Click.

He tried again. Nothing happened.

"Aw, shucks!" Donald cried. "I remembered to buy flashlights—but I forgot to buy batteries!"

Suddenly, a flash of lightning lit up the sky.

"Maybe we should just go home," Minnie said. "We can't camp in the rain without tents."

"Or dinner," added Daisy.

"Or a campfire," Goofy chimed in.

"Or a flashlight," Donald said.

Mickey agreed and the group rushed to the car.

No one spoke for the whole drive home. Mickey could tell that his friends were very disappointed.

As they walked into his house, Mickey had an idea. "I know!" he
said. "Instead of having a campout, let's have a camp-in! We can camp
right here in the living room."

"Oh, Mickey, what a great idea!" Minnie cried. "That sounds like
so much fun!"

Mickey got the tent poles from the basement. Then he put up the tents while Goofy built a fire in the fireplace.

Meanwhile, Donald found some extra batteries. In the kitchen,
Minnie and Daisy made an even better picnic dinner.

Outside, the rain kept pouring down, but Mickey and his friends didn't mind. Their tents were strong and sturdy. The fire was warm and toasty. The flashlights shined brightly. And their picnic was delicious!